JOHN & KATHERINE PATERSON
BLUEBERRIES FOR THE QUEEN

ILLUSTRATED BY SUSAN JEFFERS

HarperCollins*Publishers*

"Abracadabra!" said William, waving the broomstick over his big brother Roger. "You are now a toad."

"Stop living in a fairy tale, William," Roger said. "There's a war on."

"I know," said William, "but suppose I could wave a magic wand and turn Hitler into a loathsome toad? That would win the war all right."

"That is just plain stupid," said Roger. "Wars are won by brave, hard-working people, not by magic, and certainly not by babies like you."

All of William's family did war work. Dad worked in a factory
and Mom helped at the Red Cross.

Even Roger worked on Mr. Worth's farm, growing vegetables for the army. That left only William. He was too young to do anything to help win the war.

At night, before he fell asleep,
William imagined that he was a brave
knight winning battle after battle until
the war was over. But when morning came,
he was just William again.

One day Roger ran into the house. "Guess what? A queen has moved into the Lloyds' place! I saw her car go past. It was black and about a mile long."

"You can't fool me," said William. "There aren't any real queens in America."

"Oh, she's come, has she?" Mom sounded all excited. "She *is* a real queen, William. She's Queen Wilhelmina. She and her family had to leave the Netherlands because of the war. They're renting the Lloyd estate this summer."

"Maybe we should go visit the queen," said William.

Roger hooted. "You think you can just knock on the door and say, 'Howdy do, Mrs. Queen, I'm William Arnold from down the road'? Besides, you wouldn't know a real queen if you saw one."

"I would, too," said William. "They got robes and scepters and wear crowns on their heads."

Roger nearly fell over laughing. "And they ride in coaches made from pumpkins!"

"Of course not," said William. "That's only 'once upon a time.' Now they ride in big black cars."

William really wanted to see the queen. Every day he watched the road for her car. Did she always wear her crown? Or did she have to go about in disguise so her enemies wouldn't know who she was?

At last one day he saw a long black limousine. He waved and waved as it went by and stared as hard as he could, but the windows of the car were dark and he couldn't see anyone inside.

In the garden the squash flowers turned into baby squashes, and then into bigger ones.

The tomatoes grew fat and red. The beans hung like green tassels from their bushes.

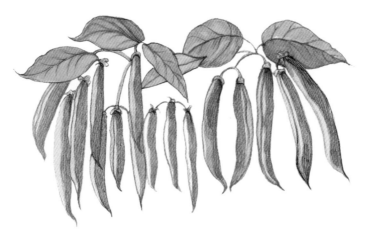

Best of all, over in the south field the blueberries began to ripen. William could hardly wait until they were ready to pick.

In the meantime, Roger almost saw the queen twice. One day, just after Roger had been there, she walked into Pease's Drugstore and asked for a sponge and a bar of soap.

"I was practically there," said Roger at supper. "I hadn't been gone more than five minutes."

A few days later Roger heard that the queen had just strolled up to a neighbor to say hello while he was working in his garden.

Why didn't the queen come strolling through his blueberry field to say hello to him? William wondered. Probably because he was just a kid not big enough to help win the war.

When the blueberries were finally ripe, William and
Dad picked blueberries all morning long. Dad put a fat
berry in his mouth. "Yum," he said. "Taste one,
William. See if it doesn't make your mouth rejoice."

William popped a handful of the sweet berries into
his mouth. "Is picking blueberries war work, Daddy?"

"No," said Dad, "I think it's more like peace work.
Nobody could be unhappy eating blueberries. They
chase all your worries away."

Just then a long black car went past. "There's the
queen's car, Dad."

"Have you seen her yet, son?"

"No," said William, "and Roger says they're leaving
soon." All summer William had lived just down the
road from a real queen, and he'd probably never even
get to see the tip of her scepter. "Roger says they're just
going to Canada. They can't go home yet."

Dad shook his head. "No, not yet. War is a terrible
thing, even for a queen."

William thought about the queen for a long time.
When bad things happened to neighbors, Mom took
them something good to eat. He got up early the next
morning and picked a basket of the biggest, bluest
berries in the patch. After breakfast he put on his best
shirt and started out the door.

"Where do you think you're going, William?" Roger
asked.

"Just out," he said. He gave Dad a wink. "I got some
peace work to do."

Roger followed him into the yard. "I'm warning you.

There's a guard at the end of the driveway. He won't
let you anywhere near the queen."

William pretended not to hear. Roger grabbed his
arm. A big juicy berry rolled off the top of the basket
and bounced on the road. "Look what you made me
do!" William chased down the berry and rubbed it on
the back of his pants.

"Look at him! Taking dirty berries to the queen!"
Roger was holding his stomach and laughing like crazy.
It was William's chance. He held the basket as steady
as he could and hurried down the road.

When he got to the Lloyd estate, a guard stepped out of a little house made from the school bus shelter. William clutched his basket tighter. The big man smiled. "Mmm, blueberries," he said.

"You can taste one," said William, "but they're really for the queen."

The soldier picked out a fat berry. "Fit for a queen,"
he said. "Just a minute." He stepped into his little
house and talked into a telephone.

"The cook says you can bring them up to the kitchen
yourself," he said. "Just follow the driveway to the side
door."

William followed the winding drive through the evergreens up to the house. The cook was waiting for him, but just as she was about to take the berries from William, another woman appeared behind her shoulder.

"What do we have here, Mrs. Watson?"

The cook gave a little bow and stepped back. "It's one of the boys from the neighborhood, ma'am, bringing some blueberries."

"I— I picked them this morning to give to the queen," said William.

"How nice!" the lady said. "What beautiful berries."

"You can taste one," said William, "but they're really for the queen."

The lady took a berry. "Lovely," she said. "I think the queen needs a nice surprise today. Why don't you come with me?"

William followed the lady through a long corridor until they reached a large, sun-filled room.

A soldier standing inside the door snapped to attention when he saw William and the lady.

"We need to see her majesty," she said. "It will only take a moment."

The soldier went into the room, bent over, and whispered something to someone William couldn't quite see.

"Excuse me, gentlemen," a woman's voice said. "My daughter needs to interrupt us for just a minute."

The men jumped to their feet and turned toward the door. William's mouth fell open. One of the men had four stars on his shoulder. He was a real general.

"A neighbor lad has brought you a gift, Mother. I thought you might like to thank him yourself."

"Of course. I'm sure the war will wait. Come in."

Hardly daring to look at the general, William made his way across the wide room. There sat a plump, white-haired lady in a regular old dress.

"What's your name, son?" the woman asked, and smiled at him just as his own grandmother would have.

If this was the queen, she wasn't at all scary, but his voice shook a little bit all the same. "I'm William," he said. "I live just down the road. I picked these blueberries in our field this morning because I . . . I . . . didn't want you to be sad . . . and . . ." But he couldn't think of anything else to say. He just held out his basket of blueberries.

"Why, thank you, William," the queen said. "No one has brought me such a nice present since I left home."

"You can taste one now if you want to," said William. "It will make your mouth rejoice."

The queen selected a big juicy berry from William's basket and put it into her mouth. Then she smiled. "You're right, William," she said. "Blueberries do make your mouth rejoice. Here, gentlemen," she said, holding out the basket to each of her guests. "Have a taste of William's blueberries." Then she handed the basket to her daughter. "Juliana, please ask Cook to serve William's berries for tea."

William knew it was time to go. "Well," he said, "good-bye, Queen." He didn't know if he should bow or not, so he just smiled.

"Good-bye, William," she said. "Thank you again for the blueberries."

William followed Princess Juliana slowly back through
the house and then walked, solemn as a knight, down the
driveway. He waved at the guard as he went past, but as
soon as he was out of sight, he broke into a run.

Roger was waiting by the driveway. "What happened?"
he asked, but William ran right past him to the house.

Dad was waiting for him at the door. "How did your
peace work go, son?" he asked.

"Great," said William. "I met a real princess and a
real general and I gave my blueberries to the queen."

"I don't believe you saw the queen," said Roger.
"It's just one of your fairy tales."

"I did so see the queen," said William. "She was
disguised like a grandma, but anyone would know she
was a real queen."

That night, as he lay in bed, William pretended that he was a mighty knight whose brave acts ended the war. "Now," he said to the queen, "we have won the war and you can go home."

The queen smiled. "Thank you, William," she said. "The war is over, but there is still a lot of peace work to be done. Can we count on you?"

William gave a deep bow. "Yes, Queen," he said. He knew he was good at peace work.

HISTORICAL NOTE

During the summer of 1942, Queen Wilhelmina of the Netherlands rented the John Bross Lloyd estate, just outside Lee, Massachusetts. Her daughter, Princess Juliana, and two granddaughters, Beatrix, age four and a half (the present queen), and Irene, age three, were with her. The stories about the queen's trip to the drugstore and her visit with the neighboring farmer are true. And there really was a little boy who brought her blueberries that summer. His name was John Paterson, and his aunt and uncle owned a house near the Lloyd estate. On a trip from his home in Connecticut, John brought blueberries he had picked especially for the queen. Although his relatives told him he would never be able to give them to her directly, he insisted on taking them to the Lloyd estate. Not only was he invited to the house, he was ushered to the queen so he could hand her the berries himself. Many years later John remembers happily how very gracious she was.

Photo used by permission of John Paterson

Blueberries for the Queen

Text copyright © 2004 by Minna Murra, Inc.

Illustrations copyright © 2004 by Susan Jeffers

Printed in the U.S.A.

www.harperchildrens.com

Library of Congress Cataloging-in-Publication Data

Paterson, Katherine.

Blueberries for the queen / by John & Katherine Paterson ; illustrated by Susan Jeffers.—1st ed. p. cm.

Summary: In the summer of 1942, when Queen Wilhelmina of the Netherlands lives down the road from his family's house in Massachusetts, young William decides to take her some of the blueberries he has picked.

Includes historical notes.

ISBN 0-06-623942-7 — ISBN 0-06-623943-5 (lib. bdg.)

1. Wilhelmina, Queen of the Netherlands, 1880–1962—Juvenile fiction. 2. World War, 1939–1945—Massachusetts—Juvenile fiction. [1. Wilhelmina, Queen of the Netherlands, 1880–1962—Fiction. 2. World War, 1939–1945—Massachusetts—Fiction. 3. Blueberries—Fiction.]

I. Paterson, John (John Barstow) II. Jeffers, Susan, ill. III. Title.

PZ7.P273Bl 2004   [E]—dc22   2003013838

Typography by Martha Rago

1 2 3 4 5 6 7 8 9 10

❖

First Edition